CRAFT ATTACK!

PRINTING CRAFTS

Annalees Lim

Gareth Stevens
Publishing

Please visit our website, www.garethstevens.com. For a free color catalog of all our high-quality books, call toll free 1-800-542-2595 or fax 1-877-542-2596.

Library of Congress Cataloging-in-Publication Data

Lim, Annalees.
Printing crafts / by Annalees Lim.
    pages cm — (Craft attack)
Includes bibliographical references and index.
ISBN 978-1-4824-3300-5 (pbk.)
ISBN 978-1-4824-0217-9 (6-pack)
ISBN 978-1-4824-0215-5 (library binding)
1. Transfer printing—Juvenile literature. 2. Decoration and ornament—Juvenile literature. I. Title.
TT852.L56 2014
745.4—dc23
                                2013021482

First Edition

Published in 2014 by
Gareth Stevens Publishing
111 East 14th Street, Suite 349
New York, NY 10003

Copyright © 2014 Arcturus Publishing

Editors: Joe Harris and Sara Gerlings
Design: Elaine Wilkinson
Cover design: Elaine Wilkinson
Photography: Simon Pask

Printed in the United States of America

CPSIA compliance information: Batch #CW14GS: For further information contact Gareth Stevens, New York, New York at 1-800-542-2595.

CONTENTS

PERFECT PRINTING

When you hear the word "printing," what do you think of? Do you imagine your desktop printer at home or a printing press churning out thousands of newspapers? Well, think again! Printing can be a lot more fun than that.

Stop the Presses! Let's Get Printing

You don't need computers or machines to print. All that you really need are your own hands and some simple craft materials. This book is full of easy, step-by-step printing projects. So grab some paints, follow the intructions, and you will be making perfect prints every time!

Get the Look!

One of the best things about printmaking is that you can print onto just about anything. Once you understand the basics, you'll be able to transform your clothes, books, stationery, and even your room.

Keep It Clean

Getting messy is all in a day's work for a printmaker. Always lay newspaper or plastic over the surface you're working on and have a damp cloth close at hand for any small spills or splatters.

Rollers and Brushes

A good selection of paintbrushes and rollers will help you to create exciting prints. Synthetic brushes will work especially well. You will also need two different types of rollers—a fluffy roller to spread paint and a hard, rubber inking roller to spread inks and apply even pressure to create your prints.

Scissors and Craft Knives

Be careful when you use scissors. If you need to cut tougher materials such as plastic, ask an adult to help. <u>NEVER</u> use a craft knife without adult help.

Paints

For most printing, you can use acrylic or poster paints. When you are printing on clothes, bags, or shoes, you will need to use fabric paint. Carefully follow the instructions on the fabric paint itself to make sure that it will be colorfast. If the instructions say to use an iron, you should ask an adult for help.

Glue

Sometimes called white glue, this works well for sticking things like paper and wood together.

Glue Stick

This is very easy to use and great for sticking paper together.

Fabric Glue

This is great for sticking paper or cardboard to fabric.

Craft Glue or Hobby Glue

This is useful if you need to stick on hard plastic things such as buttons or googly eyes.

APPLE PRINT CANVAS BAG

Printing with fruits and vegetables is easy, and it looks great. This fruity canvas bag is perfect for making shopping trips. It saves on using plastic bags, so it's good for the environment!

You will need:

- blank canvas bag
- apples
- fabric paint
- table knife
- plastic cutting board
- paintbrushes

1 Cut some apples in half. You may want to ask an adult to help.

2 Brush a thin layer of fabric paint onto a plastic cutting board.

3 Press the flat part of the apple onto the paint, making sure that the whole flat surface of the apple is covered.

4 Firmly press the apple onto the canvas bag. When you lift it off, you will reveal an apple-shaped print!

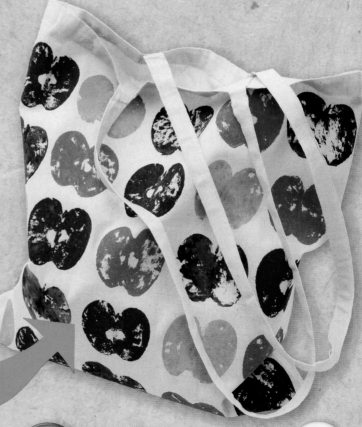

5 Repeat steps 3 and 4 until you have covered the whole bag, changing colors if you like. Leave to dry. Then check the instructions on your fabric paint. If the instructions say that you should use an iron to set the paint, ask an adult to help you.

BLOCK PRINTED CARDS

Relief prints are usually made by cutting into wood. Here's how you can create the same effect with craft foam!

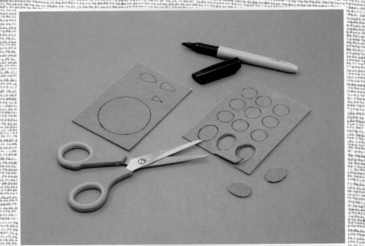

1 Draw shapes onto craft foam, and cut them out with scissors. For a bee, you will need a large oval, two teardrop shapes, a triangle, and a small circle. For flowers, you will need three large circles and eight small ones.

2 Cut each of the small circles in half. Cut the large oval into three parts, and snip into one part to give your bee an eye and a mouth.

3 Stick the shapes onto the wooden block using craft glue. Leave them to dry.

4 Paint or roller a thin layer of paint onto the block. Then press it onto the card.

5 Carefully peel off the block to reveal your design. Repeat steps 4 and 5 if you would like to print more cards!

ONE-OFF PORTRAIT PRINT

Here is a project that makes only one final print. It can never be repeated, so it is unique! This type of printing is called a monoprint. A monoprint portrait makes a great gift.

1 Using a brush, paint a brightly colored rectangle onto your plastic cutting board.

2 Now paint a frame around your rectangle in different colors.

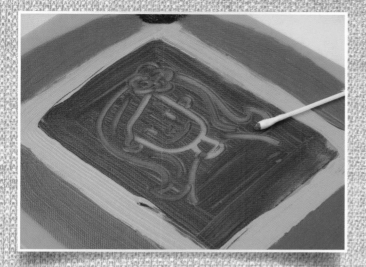

3 Leave this for a couple of minutes so that it begins to dry, and then draw the outline of your portrait, using a cotton swab. Make sure that you press firmly!

4 Use the cotton swab to draw some patterns onto your painted frame.

5 Carefully lay a piece of paper onto your board. Press it down gently all over. Then lift it off to reveal your print!

FUNKY PATTERN PRINTS

Here is a good way of printing repeating patterns. When you have finished making your print, you can frame it and hang it on the wall.

You will need:

a styrofoam plate
black marker
tracing paper
blunt pencil
paints and paper
foam roller
printing roller
tape
scissors

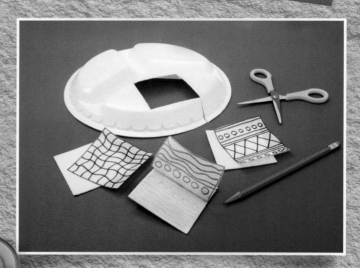

1 Draw some squares on a plain piece of paper using a black marker. Decorate each square with a different pattern. Cut out the squares with scissors.

2 Now cut some squares of the same size from your styrofoam plate. Place the paper squares on top of your styrofoam squares. Trace the lines using a blunt pencil. Push hard, to make deep grooves.

3 Use the foam roller to cover the styrofoam squares with a thin layer of paint. If you don't have a foam roller, you could use a normal paintbrush.

4 Starting in the top left-hand corner of your paper, place the styrofoam down and use the printing roller to apply firm and even pressure. If you don't have a printing roller, you could use a rolling pin wrapped in plastic wrap.

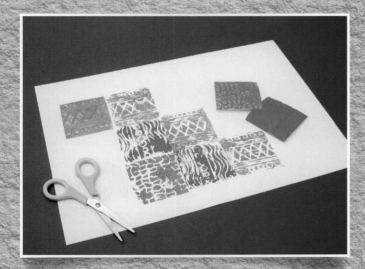

5 Remove the styrofoam to reveal your print. Repeat steps 4 and 5 again and again to make more prints on your paper. Leave your print to dry, then cut it out.

STENCIL ART PLANT POT

Because the stencils in this project are flexible, you can use them to print on curved surfaces! You will need an adult to help you with cutting out the stencils. Never use a craft knife without adult supervision.

You will need:
paper
black marker
2 sheets of acetate
craft knife
paint
clay plant pot
brush
masking tape

1 Draw your design onto a piece of paper.

2 Trace the lines of your drawing onto tracing paper, but leave little spaces in the lines. Then trace the outline onto a separate piece of tracing paper, and color it in.

3 Trace the spaced-line drawing and the outline drawing onto an acetate sheet. Ask an adult to cut out everything colored black on the acetate sheets with a craft knife.

4 Stick the stencil with the larger cut-out areas to the clay pot, using your masking tape.

5 Paint everything inside the template area blue and leave to dry.

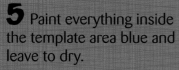

6 Now tape the other stencil over the top and use white paint to add the final layer to your design. Wait for it to dry.

CLAY PRINTING

You can make prints *in* wet clay and make prints *from* wet clay! This double printing method makes beautiful pictures. The prints look best when the clay is still wet, so you have to work fast!

You will need:
air-drying clay
clay tools
(or ordinary cutlery)
rolling pin
string
printing roller
foam roller
paint
sturdy paper

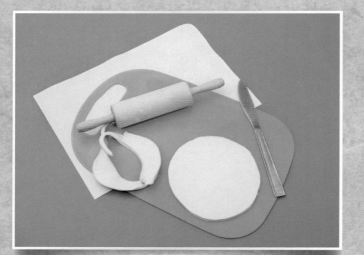

1 Roll out your clay so that you have a piece that is 0.4 inch (1 cm) thick and smaller than your piece of paper.

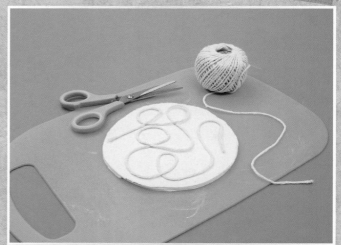

2 Place your string on top of the clay in an interesting pattern. Press down to make an imprint before you remove it.

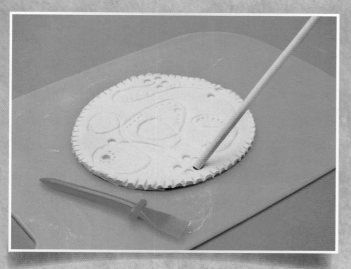

3 Use clay tools (or a knife and fork) to add more details in the clay.

4 Roll a thin layer of paint onto the clay.

5 Place a piece of paper on top, and use either another roller or your hands to press it down.

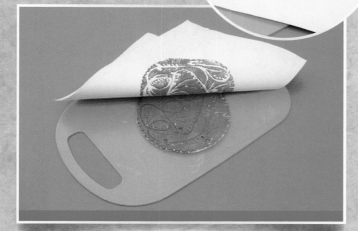

6 Remove the paper to reveal your print.

When you have finished your prints, make a hole at the top of the Clay slab before leaving it to dry. When the Clay has hardened you can hang it up as a plaque!

ROLLER PRINT FOLDERS

Rolling pin prints make excellent repeat patterns. You never know quite what they will look like until you have started to roll! You can use this technique to personalize your school binders.

You will need

- plastic wrap
- rolling pin
- card stock
- self-adhesive craft foam sheets
- scissors
- blank non-glossy, 3-ring binder
- acrylic paint
- plastic cutting board
- tape

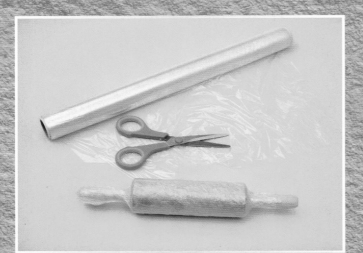

1 Cover the whole rolling pin with some plastic wrap.

2 Cut out a piece of card stock that will fit around the rolling pin, and attach it using a piece of tape.

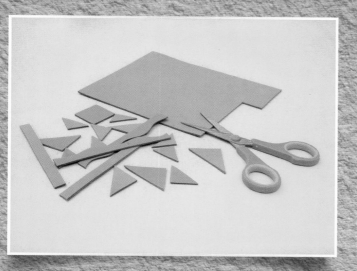

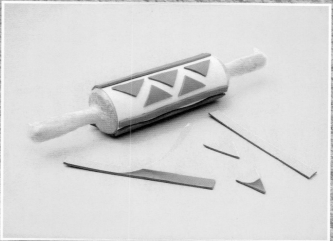

3 Cut out lots of shapes from your craft foam, using scissors. You will need enough shapes to cover nearly all of the rolling pin.

4 Peel off the backing from the craft foam and stick it onto the rolling pin. You will need to make sure that you space them evenly to make a print without big gaps.

5 Spread an even layer of paint onto the cutting board, and roll the rolling pin through the paint.

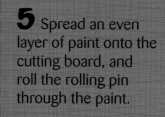

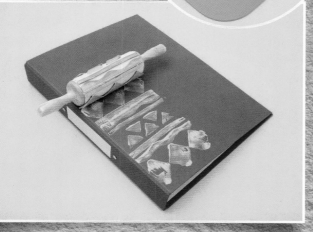

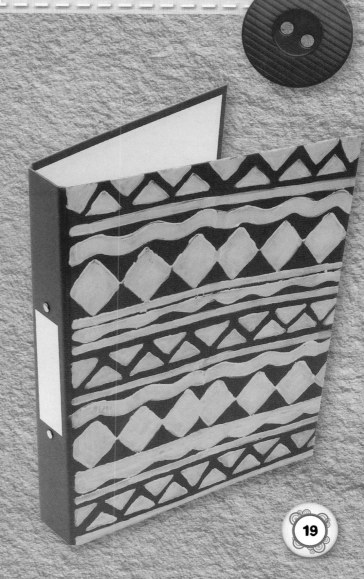

6 Roll the rolling pin over your folder to create a repeat pattern. You may want to practice on a piece of scrap paper first.

PLASTIC WRAP WRAPPING PAPER

Plastic wrap may be good for wrapping up food, but it's also great for craft projects. This cool wrapping paper will really make your gifts stand out from the rest!

You will need

plastic cutting board
plastic wrap
aluminium foil
paper and scissors
poster paint and silver paint
paintbrushes

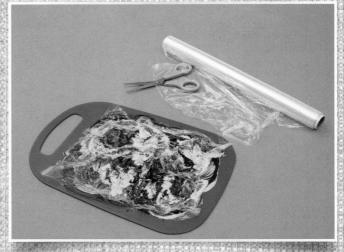

1 Spread three colors of paint onto your cutting board, swirling them together with your paintbrush to make a pattern.

2 Put a square of plastic wrap onto the paint mixture and press it down.

3 Carefully lift the plastic wrap and lower it onto your paper. You do not want it to be a flat print so it doesn't matter if it scrunches up. Lift off the plastic wrap to reveal your pattern.

4 Repeat steps 2 and 3 until you have covered the whole piece of paper. Leave to dry.

5 For some added sparkle, paint the cutting board with silver paint. Scrunch up some aluminium foil and press it onto the silver paint. Then press it onto the paper.

BUTTON PRINT SNEAKERS

Here is how you can make your old sneakers look fresh and exciting! This type of printing uses found objects. If you don't want to use buttons or don't have any on hand, you can try using bottle caps instead.

You will need

bottle corks
buttons
craft glue
old plain-colored canvas sneakers
fabric paint, paintbrush and palette
thin black marker

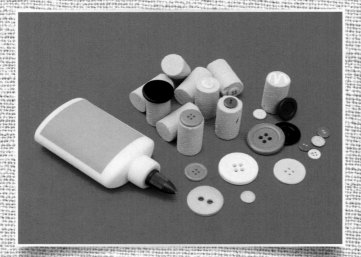

1 Glue some buttons onto the top of bottle corks, using craft glue. Leave them to dry.

2 Use a paintbrush to paint a layer of fabric paint onto one of the button stamps.

3 Press the stamp onto the sneaker and lift it off to reveal your print. Repeat with all the other button stamps and cover your sneakers with lots of prints.

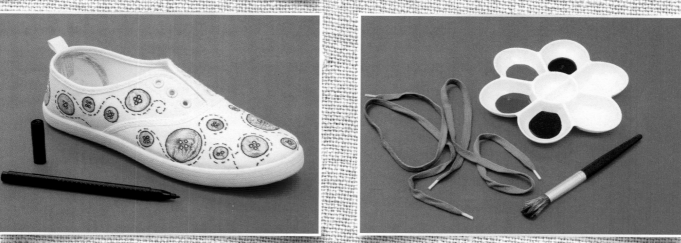

4 Add to your design using a thin black marker.

5 Paint the laces in a bright color and leave them to dry. Finally, check the instructions for your fabric paint. If you need to use an iron to set the paint, ask an adult to help.

23

EASY SCREEN PRINTS

Screen printing is similar to stencil printing, except that the ink is pushed through a mesh using a tool called a squeegee. If you do not have a squeegee, try using a plastic card instead.

You will need

wooden frame (an old photo frame will work)
straight pins
voile (fine netting)
glue
paint and paintbrush
plastic card
paper and pencil
black marker

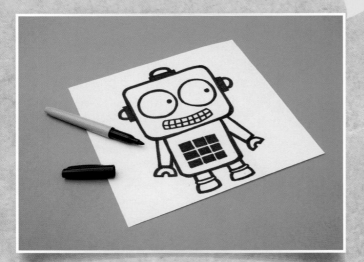

1 Draw a pattern or illustration onto a piece of paper, using bold, heavy lines.

2 Stretch some voile netting across a frame, and ask an adult to pin it in place.

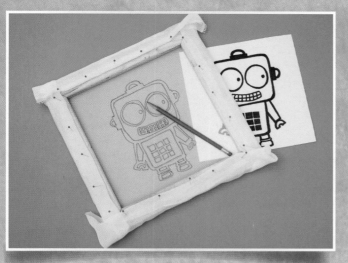

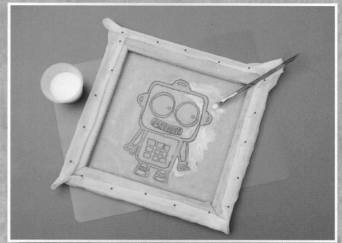

3 Trace around the outside of the black lines in your design onto the netting, using a fine pencil line.

4 First, protect your surface! Paint over the whole screen with glue, except for the areas inside your pencil lines. Do the same to the other side. Leave it to dry.

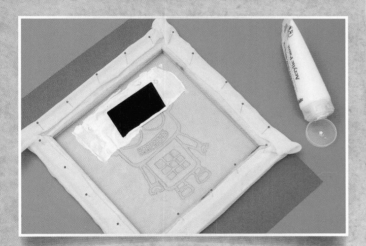

5 Place the screen on top of a piece of colored paper. Ask someone to hold it in place for you. Brush some paint across the top of the netting, then use a plastic card to drag the paint across the screen. When you have finished, take another piece of paper, and repeat as many times as you like. Finally, cut around your prints with scissors.

SPOTTY PAINTED MUGS

Breakfast will never be dull again with this personalized mug. But beware, once you have a mug that looks this good, everyone will want to use it!

You will need

- ceramic paints
- pencil and marker pen
- plain mug
- carbon paper
- paper
- scissors
- masking tape
- cotton swab

1 Measure around your mug, then measure the height and cut a piece of paper to the same size. Use this to draw your design onto.

2 Tape some carbon paper onto the mug, and then tape your design on top of that.

3 Trace over your design with a pencil, pressing hard. Then remove the papers from the mug to reveal a faint print.

4 Start to paint on the mug by dabbing on ceramic paint with a cotton swab.

5 Keep stippling (dotting) on the ceramic paint until you have finished your picture! Then you will need to follow the instructions on the label of your ceramic paint to make it set. Most ceramic paints will need to be baked in the oven.

WARNING!

If the instructions for the ceramic paint tell you to use the oven, ask an adult to help. Don't do this on your own!

BUBBLE PRINT T-SHIRT

Don't pop it, print it! Bubble wrap makes fun, spotty prints. Your friends will be impressed when they see your bubble print T-shirt!

You will need:
bubble wrap
scissors
fabric paint
blank T-shirt
plastic cutting board
paintbrushes

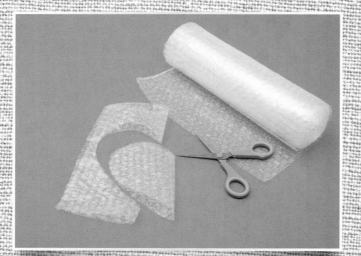

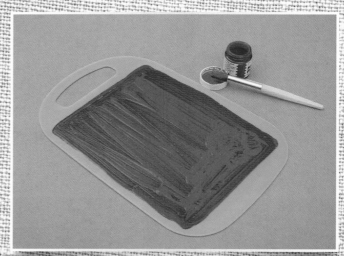

1 Fold a piece of bubble wrap in half and cut out a teardrop shape, as shown above. When you unfold it, it will make a heart.

2 Paint a thin layer of red paint onto the plastic cutting board.

3 Add some other colors of paint to the pallet, using a paintbrush.

4 Lay the outer part of the bubble wrap down in the paint. Press it down firmly.

5 Transfer the bubble wrap onto the T-shirt, and press it down firmly. Lift the bubble wrap to reveal the print! Leave it to dry. Then repeat steps 3 to 5 with the heart shape and a different color of paint. Finally, check the instructions for your fabric paint. If you need to use an iron to set the paint, ask an adult to help.

SANDPAPER PRINTING

You may think that sandpaper is only good for making things smooth... but think again! It's great for making one-off prints onto fabric too. We've used this technique to decorate a pencil case.

You will need

medium coarse sandpaper
crayons
iron
plain fabric pencil case
cardboard
kitchen towel or piece of fabric
scissors

1 Cut a piece of sandpaper to the same shape as the pencil case. Draw a design on it, using colored crayons.

2 Keep adding to your picture to fill the whole space. Make sure that you press down firmly, to create a thick layer of wax.

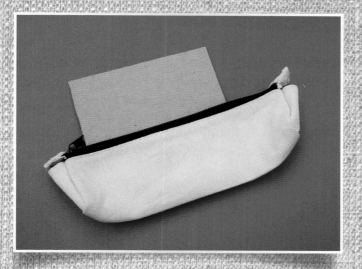

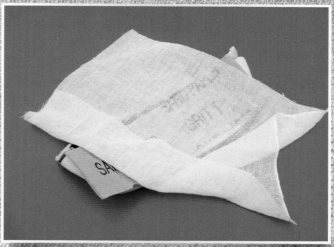

3 Place a piece of cardboard underneath the fabric that you are going to transfer the pattern onto. We've placed it inside the pencil case.

4 Place your sandpaper onto your fabric with the pattern facing down. Cover it with a kitchen towel or piece of fabric.

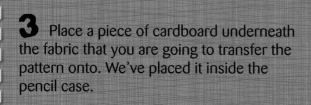

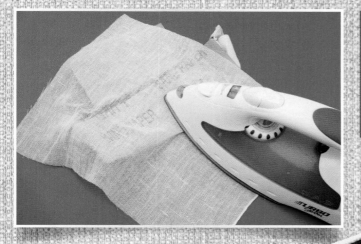

5 Ask an adult to iron over the sandpaper for 2 to 3 minutes. Then lift it off to reveal the pattern on your pencil case!

GLOSSARY

acetate A transparent sheet of plastic.

relief printing A printing technique where raised shapes or letters are covered in ink, before being pressed onto a surface.

stencil printing A printing technique where ink or paint is pushed through a pattern that has been cut into a sheet of plastic, cardboard, or metal.

stippling A technique in drawing or painting where the artist makes a series of small dots or marks.

FURTHER READING

Ed Emberley's Complete Funprint Drawing Book by Ed Emberley (Little, Brown, 2005)

Stencil Art by Paula Hannigan (Klutz, 2007)

The Usborne Book of Art Skills by Fiona Watt (Usborne Publishing Ltd, 2008)

WEBSITES

kids.nationalgeographic.co.uk/kids/activities/crafts/
Crafts inspired by nature.

spoonful.com/crafts
Crafts and activities for a range of ages.

www.firstpalette.com
A range of bright and colorful crafts for every occasion.

INDEX